Sofi and the Magic, Musical Mural

Sofi y el mágico mural musical

By / Por
Raquel M. Ortiz

Illustrations by / Ilustraciones de
Maria Dominguez

Spanish translation by / Traducción al español de
Gabriela Baeza Ventura

Piñata Books
Arte Público Press
Houston, Texas

Publication of *Sofi and the Magic, Musical Mural* is funded by a grant from the City of Houston through the Houston Arts Alliance. We are grateful for their support.

Esta edición de *Sofi y el mágico mural musical* ha sido subvencionada por la ciudad de Houston a través de la Houston Arts Alliance. Les agradecemos su apoyo.

Piñata Books are full of surprises!
¡Piñata Books están llenos de sorpresas!

Piñata Books
An Imprint of Arte Público Press
University of Houston
4902 Gulf Fwy, Bldg 19, Rm 100
Houston, Texas 77204-2004

Cover design by / Diseño de la portada por Bryan Dechter.

Ortiz, Raquel M., author.
    Sofi and the magic, musical mural / by Raquel M. Ortiz ; illustrations by Maria Dominguez ; Spanish translation by Gabriela Baeza Ventura = Sofi y el mágico mural musical / por Raquel M. Ortiz ; ilustraciones de Maria Dominguez ; traducción al español de Gabriela Baeza Ventura.
        p. cm.
    Summary: On the way back from the bodega, Sofía is drawn into a life-like mural of Old San Juan where she dances, sings and conquers her fear of the vejigante before being called back to the barrio by her mother.
    ISBN 978-1-55885-803-9 (alk. paper)
    [1. Mural painting and decoration—Fiction. 2. Fear—Fiction. 3. Dance—Fiction. 4. San Juan (P.R.)—History—Fiction.] I. Dominguez, Maria, 1950- illustrator. II. Ventura, Gabriela Baeza, translator. III. Title. IV. Title: Sofi y el mágico mural musical.
PZ73.O717 2015
[E]—dc23
                                                                    014037794
                                                                    CIP

♾ The paper used in this publication meets the requirements of the American National Standard for Permanence of Paper for Printed Library Materials Z39.48-1984.

Printed in China in October 2014–January 2015 by Creative Printing USA Inc.
12 11 10 9 8 7 6 5 4 3 2 1

To Fifi and Che, who help me make art and tell stories.
To Dr. José Antonio González Alcantud and Dr. Alberto Hernández,
who help people realize their dreams.
—RMO

To my husband for his continued support, love and patience.
—MD

Para Fifi y Che, quienes me ayudan a hacer arte y a contar historias.
Para los doctores José Antonio González Alcantud y Alberto
Hernández, quienes ayudan a la gente a cumplir sus sueños.
—RMO

Para mi esposo por su constante apoyo, cariño y paciencia.
—MD

Sofía was lying on her bed, looking up at the ceiling. She was soooo bored when Mami walked in and said, "Sofi, please go to the bodega and get us some milk."

"Okay, let me get my shoes on."

Sofía estaba acostada en su cama, mirando el techo. Estaba tan pero tan aburrida cuando Mami entró y dijo —Sofi, por favor ve a comprar leche a la bodega.

—Está bien, deja que me ponga los zapatos.

As Sofía walked into the living room to get her scarf and coat, Mami began the usual speech, "Now remember, don't talk to ANYONE! Go straight to the store and back."

Sofía nodded and wrapped the scarf around her neck. She knew her mom would be watching from the apartment window as she walked all the way to the store at the end of the block.

En cuanto Sofía entró a la sala para agarrar la bufanda y el abrigo, Mami empezó con lo mismo de siempre —Y recuerda, ¡no hables con naaaadie! Ve derechito a la bodega y de vuelta a casa.

Sofía asintió y se puso la bufanda en el cuello. Sabía que su mamá la observaría desde la ventana del departamento hasta la tienda, al final de la cuadra.

Once outside, Sofía looked at the mural painted on a building. It was huge! Even from across the street she could see everything: musicians, dancers, tropical fish, a large *amapola* flower and–her least favorite–a *vejigante*. She knew that the *vejigante* was just a trickster who danced around people, trying to hit them with a *vejiga*, a little bag. But, when Sofía looked at the sneaky smile on the *vejigante* mask and its three horns, she was glad it was just a painting.

Una vez afuera, Sofía miró hacia el mural que estaba pintado en un edificio. ¡Era grandísimo! Desde el otro lado de la calle podía ver todo: músicos, bailarines, peces tropicales, una amapola gigante y lo que menos le gustaba, un vejigante. Sabía que el vejigante era un bromista que bailaba alrededor de la gente, tratando de pegarle con una vejiga o una bolsita. Pero, cuando Sofía vio la sonrisa pícara y los tres cuernos en la máscara del vejigante, se alegró de que sólo fuera una pintura.

At the *bodega,* Sofía bought a half-gallon of milk and quickly left the store. She decided to cross the street to walk by the mural. As Sofía made her way back home, she noticed how life-like everything looked. The colorful tropical fish swimming past her in the warm Caribbean Sea made the wintery day a little less dreary. When she came to the musicians, the *pleneros,* she stopped. One had his hand held out and seemed to be inviting her to dance. Sofía put down the milk and said with a giggle, "Okay, let's dance."

En la bodega, Sofía compró medio galón de leche y rápidamente salió de la tienda. Decidió cruzar la calle para caminar cerca del mural. Mientras caminaba de regreso a casa, descubrió que todo parecía más real. Los peces tropicales que se alejaban nadando en el cálido mar del Caribe hicieron que el día de invierno fuera menos gris. Cuando llegó a los pleneros, se detuvo. Uno tenía la mano extendida, como invitándola a bailar. Sofía puso la leche en el suelo y con una risita dijo —Está bien, bailemos.

Suddenly, Sofía found herself in the middle of Viejo San Juan, on the island of Puerto Rico, surrounded by the music of tambourines, bongos, maracas and *güiros.*

"W-W-W-What's going on?" stuttered Sofía.

"Well, you said you wanted to dance!" her new friend said.

Sofía, too shocked to do anything else, began to dance.

De repente, Sofía se encontró en medio del Viejo San Juan, en la isla de Puerto Rico, rodeada del ritmo de la pandereta, los bongós, las maracas y los güiros.

—¿Qué es lo que está pa-pasando? —Sofía tartamudeó.

—Bueno, ¡dijiste que querías bailar! —dijo su nuevo amigo.

Sofía estaba demasiado sorprendida como para hacer otra cosa y empezó a bailar.

Before she knew it, a group of musicians and dancers made a circle around them. They were singing a famous *plena* song:

"The *plena* music that I know

is not from China, it comes from home.

Because the *plena* was born in Ponce

it's from the barrio of San Antón."

Antes de que se diera cuenta, un grupo de músicos y bailarines les hicieron una ronda. Todos estaban cantando la famosa plena:

"La plena que yo conozco

no es de la China ni del Japón.

Porque la plena viene de Ponce,

viene del barrio de San Antón".

Soon, Sofía joined in the chorus as she danced.

After the song ended, the musicians began to play a song from carnival. Sofía didn't even have a chance to catch her breath.

"Toco-toco, toco-toco, Vejigante eating coconut!

Toco-toco, toco-toco, Vejigante eating coconut!"

De un momento a otro, Sofía empezó a cantar mientras bailaba.

Cuando terminó la canción, los músicos empezaron a tocar una canción de carnaval. Sofía ni tuvo oportunidad de tomarse un descansito.

"¡Toco-toco, toco-toco! ¡Vejigante come coco!

¡Toco-toco, toco-toco! ¡Vejigante come coco!"

Out of nowhere came a person dressed in a black jumper with yellow ruffles and a red mask made from a coconut shell. It was the *vejigante* from the mural! Sofía tried to make a run for it, but her dance partner stopped her, "Don't be afraid. Nothing's going to happen."

But Sofía was sure something bad would happen when the scary-looking *vejigante* took her hand. Sofía wanted to scream! But, instead she tried to avoid getting hit by the trickter's bag.

De la nada salió un personaje vestido con un mameluco negro y volantes amarillos y una máscara roja hecha con un coco. ¡Era el vejigante del mural! Sofía intentó correr, pero su pareja de baile la detuvo —No tengas miedo. No va a pasar nada.

Pero Sofía estaba segura de que algo le pasaría cuando el vejigante le tomó la mano. ¡Sofía quería gritar! Pero mejor buscó cómo evitar que la golpeara con la vejiga.

The *vejigante* began to spin-spin-spin Sofía. When the spinning was finally over, a dizzy Sofía discovered she was now dressed as a *vejigante*! She touched her face. It was covered with the three-horned mask! Her black jumper had a brilliant yellow ruffle!

Now the musicians began to sing to her:

"*Vejigante* just wants to play!

In red and yellow she'll have her way!"

El vejigante empezó a darle vueltas y vueltas y más vueltas a Sofía. Cuando por fin se detuvo, Sofía estaba mareada y descubrió que ella ¡ahora estaba disfrazada de vejigante! Se tocó la cara. ¡Estaba cubierta con la máscara de tres cuernos! Su mameluco ¡tenía brillantes holanes amarillos!

Los músicos ahora le cantaban a ella:

"Vejigante está pintao

de amarillo y colorao".

Laughing, Sofía started to dance around the church plaza lightly tapping everyone with the *vejiga*. Then, she opened her arms and began to spin around, the ruffles billowing around her. She spun faster and faster, keeping time with the music.

Before she knew what had happened, Sofía was above the dancers and musicians. She was flying! Sofía looked back and waved goodbye as she left the street party. Everyone cheered as she went soaring through the air.

Riendo, Sofía empezó a bailar por la plaza de la iglesia y a darles golpes suavecitos con la vejiga a todos. Después, abrió los brazos y comenzó a dar vueltas con los volantes ondulando a su alrededor. Dio vueltas más rápidas, manteniendo el ritmo de la música.

Sin darse cuenta, Sofía estaba por encima de los danzantes y músicos. ¡Estaba volando! Sofía miró hacia atrás y se despidió de la fiesta en la calle. Todos la animaron mientras volaba por el cielo.

First, Sofía soared eastward to visit El Yunque, the rain forest. She heard the gurgling of the waterfalls and the chatter of the parrots. Then, Sofía flew over lush mountain vegetation that seemed to go on forever.

After getting her fill of crisp mountain air, Sofía glided south toward the beach, where she could make out the figures of vibrant fish and spiky coral in the sapphire blue Caribbean Sea. The salty water called out to her, and she came closer and closer to the foamy white waves, ready to plunge in . . .

Primero, Sofía voló hacia el este para visitar El Yunque, el bosque lluvioso. Escuchó el borboteo de las cascadas y el cotorreo de los loros. Luego, Sofía voló por encima de la abundante vegetación de las montañas que parecía no acabar nunca.

Después de llenarse del fresco aire de las montañas, Sofía se deslizó al sur, hacia la playa, en donde pudo ver las siluetas de los animados peces y el coral puntiagudo en el agua azul zafiro del mar Caribe. El agua salada la llamaba y ella se acercó más y más a las espumosas olas blancas, lista para zambullirse . . .

"Sofi, what's wrong? I've been calling and calling you and all you've done is stand here, staring at this mural. What's going on?" Mami asked, annoyed.

Startled, Sofía looked down at herself. She was no longer clad in a colorful *vejigante* outfit.

"Mami, I'm sorry, I was just looking at the mural and . . . " she muttered as she bent to pick up the milk.

—Sofi, ¿qué te pasa? Te he estado llamando y llamando, pero lo único que has hecho es quedarte parada aquí, mirando fijamente el mural. ¿Qué te pasa? —preguntó Mami, molesta.

Sorprendida, Sofía se miró la ropa. Ya no llevaba el colorido disfraz de vejigante.

—Lo siento, Mami, sólo estaba mirando el mural y . . . —musitó al agacharse para levantar la leche.

Sofía took her mom's hand and started walking home. She glanced at the mural one last time to admire her sister's name, Esmeralda Pagán, on the long list of students who had helped paint the mural. Silently, Sofía and her mom climbed up the two flights of stairs.

Sofía tomó la mano de su mamá, y empezaron a caminar a casa. Dio una última mirada al mural para admirar el nombre de su hermana, Esmeralda Pagán, en la larga lista de estudiantes que ayudaron a pintarlo. Sofía y su mamá subieron los dos pisos de escaleras en silencio.

Back in her apartment, Sofía went to her bedroom window and looked at the mural across the street, "The Pueblo Sings." Now, the *vejigante* didn't seem so scary. Staring at the mural, she could have sworn she saw the *vejigante* wink!

"Maybe this really is a singing and dancing town," Sofía said to herself quietly.

Then, Sofía began to hum and dance a *plena*, her arms outstretched to her friends across the street.

De vuelta en su departamento, Sofía fue a la ventana de su cuarto y observó el mural al otro lado de la calle, "El pueblo cantor". Ya no le daba tanto miedo el vejigante. Al mirar con detenimiento el mural, ¡podría jurar que vio que el vejigante le guiñó el ojo!

—Tal vez éste sí es un pueblo cantor y bailarín —dijo Sofía para sí.

Después, Sofía se puso a tararear y bailar una plena con los brazos extendidos hacia sus amigos al otro lado de la calle.

Raquel M. Ortiz was born and raised in Lorain, Ohio, and has been making art and telling stories ever since she was a little girl. She holds a Ph.D. in Social Anthropology from the University of Salamanca and has worked at The Brooklyn Museum, the Allen Memorial Art Museum and El Museo del Barrio. Raquel is the author of *El arte de la identidad* (La Galera, 2011), the documentary *Memories of the Wall: Education and Enrichment through Community Murals* and textbooks and educational material for children in Puerto Rico and the United States. She lives in New York City with her family and is a professor at Boricua College.

Raquel M. Ortiz nació y se crio en Lorain, Ohio, y ha hecho arte y contado historias desde que era pequeña. Tiene un doctorado en antropología social de la Universidad de Salamanca y ha trabajado en The Brooklyn Museum, el Allen Memorial Art Museum y en El Museo del Barrio. Es autora de *El arte de la identidad* (La Galera, 2011), el documental *Memories of the Wall: Education and Enrichment through Community Murals* y libros de texto y materiales educativos para niños en Puerto Rico y Estados Unidos. Raquel vive en la ciudad de Nueva York con su familia y es profesora en Boricua College.

Maria Dominguez moved from Cataño, Puerto Rico, to New York City when she was five years old. She began her artistic career as a muralist with Cityarts in 1982; that first experience with public art showed her that people can create art together for their community. Over the past twenty-five years, Maria has created over twenty public art murals and worked with the Metropolitan Transportation Authority of New York City, Artmakers, Inc. and Brooklyn Connect. The recipient of grants from the National Endowment for the Arts and the New York Foundation for the Arts, she has also headed El Museo del Barrio's Education Department. She currently teaches art in New York City's Public School System.

Maria Dominguez se mudó de Cataño, Puerto Rico, a la ciudad de Nueva York a los cinco años. Empezó su carrera artística como muralista para Cityarts en 1982; esa primera experiencia con el arte público le enseñó que la gente puede crear arte para su comunidad. En los últimos veinticinco años, Maria ha creado más de veinte murales de arte público, y trabajado con el Metropolitan Transportation Authority de la ciudad de Nueva York, Artmakers, Inc. y Brooklyn Connect. Ha sido merecedora de becas del National Endowment for the Arts y de la New York Foundation for the Arts y supervisado el departamento de educación de El Museo del Barrio. En la actualidad da clases de arte en las escuelas públicas de la ciudad de Nueva York.

Glossary

Amapola   rosy red flower that looks like a hibiscus but grows from a tree.

Bodega   neighborhood store that carries staples and specialty items.

Bongós   percussion instrument made up of two small drums attached to each other. The drums are different sizes: the larger drum is called the *hembra* (female), the smaller drum is called the *macho* (male).

Güiro   indigenous percussion instrument that consists of an open-ended, hollow gourd with parallel notches cut in one side. It is played by rubbing a wooden stick (*rascador*) along the notches to produce a ratchet-like sound.

Pandereta   hand-held percussion instrument similar, in appearance to the tambourine, that is made out of metal and leather.

Plena   national song structure and rhythm of Puerto Rico. *Plena* is also known as the singing newspaper because it includes everyday topics.

Vejigante   descendent of the devil figure of the medieval religious dramas (a combination of traditional theater and the presentations of "Moors and Christians"). The name comes from the word *vejiga* (bladder) because traditionally he would carry an inflated cow or pig bladder, filled with water, and hit people on the head with it. The bladder is similar to the scepter used by buffoons. The medieval devils, like the buffoons, used the colors red and yellow. The *vejigante* wears masks with three horns made from coconut shells.

Information about the mural

"El pueblo cantor" (The Pueblo Sings) is a 20' x 90' mural located in the South Bronx, on the corner of Prospect and East Treemont. It was financed by Banco Popular of Puerto Rico and is painted on the wall of one of its branch offices. The objective was to create an anti-graffiti wall with the students from Intermediate School 193 (I.S. 193). The students, who were studying Puerto Rican culture, drew images that they wanted in the mural. Maria Dominguez created her design for the mural based on those drawings and on the numerous conversations that she held with the students. After the mural was designed, the 7th and 8th graders helped paint the base and create a grid for the mural. The students fully embraced the process of the community creation: they created a work of art for a local audience based on themes of interest to the community